Winston
the window-sill-sitting pumpkin

Henry
the haunted pumpkin

Pumper-Lina
the broom-riding pumpkin

Tilly
the troll's pumpkin

Jonas
the joking pumpkin

Larry
the laughing pumpkin

Pee-wee
the parade-leading
pumpkin

Patrick
the slightly poorly
pumpkin

Dolores
the dancy-eyed pumpkin

Yoshi
the YUMMY SCRUMMY

pumpkin

Mumsie
the mummy pumpkin

Dotty
the spotted pumpkin

Iggy
the INCREDIBLE
patterned pumpkin

Pip-Squeak
the itsy-bitsy
baby pumpkin

Wilbur
the WHIRLY SWIRLY pumpkin

Reuben
the REMARKABLE
patterned pumpkin

Sylvester
the SPECTACULAR
star-patterned pumpkin

Toshi
the TERRIFIC
teardrop-patterned pumpkin

Corey
the CUTEST pumpkin

Sally
the SENSATIONAL
square-patterned pumpkin

For Lonnie, Nick and Phoebe and
all the Halloweens to come – M.S.

To Iris, happy Halloween! x – T.B.

Published in the UK by Scholastic, 2023
1 London Bridge, London, SE1 9BG
Scholastic Ireland, 89E Lagan Road, Dublin Industrial Estate, Glasnevin, Dublin, D11 HP5F

SCHOLASTIC and associated logos are trademarks and/or
registered trademarks of Scholastic Inc.

Text © Mark Sperring, 2023
Illustrations © Tim Budgen, 2023

The right of Mark Sperring and Tim Budgen to be identified
as the author and illustrator of this work has been asserted by them
under the Copyright, Designs and Patents Act 1988.

ISBN 978 0702 32468 0

A CIP catalogue record for this book is available from the British Library.

Printed in China
Paper made from wood grown in sustainable forests and other controlled sources.

1 3 5 7 9 10 8 6 4 2

This is a work of fiction. Names, characters, places, incidents and dialogues are products
of the author's imagination or are used fictitiously. Any resemblance to actual people,
living or dead, events or locales is entirely coincidental.

www.scholastic.co.uk

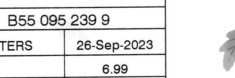

MARK SPERRING

TIM BUDGEN

20 PUMPKINS *·*· at *·*· BEDTIME

SCHOLASTIC

One spooky-wooky bat winged night, Broom-Ella could not sleep,

so, her cat and frog and owl said that she should count some sheep.

But, sheep don't shine with magic,
or possess HUGE beaming grins.

So, Broom—Ella put her spell
book down and counted . . .

BRIGHT PUMPKINS!

1...

Here's a pumpkin sitting on a window sill.

2...

Here's a pumpkin who just got a ghostly thrill!

3...

Here's a pumpkin that –
can you believe it . . .
FLEW.

4... Here's a pumpkin who heard some TROLLS shout,

"BOO!"

5... Here's a pumpkin with a joke that's OH-SO daft ...

6...

Here's a pumpkin
who just laughed
and laughed and laughed.

7...

Here's a pumpkin that
a little vampire made.

8...

Here's a pumpkin who
is leading a parade!

9...
Here's a pumpkin who watched two white mice dance by.

10...
Here's a pumpkin who became a pumpkin pie!

11...

Here's a pumpkin
whose big eyes
are filled with love.

12...

Here's a pumpkin
that is feeling
nice and snug.

Yes, once upon a pumpkin-counting, glowing, gleaming night,

Broom–Ella's very sleepy eyes
finally shut tight!

But, in her dreams, she kept on counting pumpkins that she saw. But,

13...

14...

15...

they weren't like the ones before!

16 . . .
Here's a pumpkin loudly shouting,

"TRICK OR TREAT!"

17...

Here's a pumpkin – shhh! –
who's fallen fast asleep.

19...
Here's a pumpkin who I know will sleep till dawn.

20!

Here's the CUTEST pumpkin
that Broom-Ella carved herself!

She'd made it before bedtime
and placed it on this shelf . . .

It sat here, watching over her,
as she dreamt sweet pumpkin dreams,

and filled the night
with lantern light,
one HAPPY HALLOWEEN!

11 12 13

14 16

15

17 18 20

19